FRANCES DEAN

Who Loved to Dance and Dance

TO ALL THOSE WHO LIVE
WITH ALL THEIR HEART

Copyright © 2014 by Birgitta Sif

First U.S. edition 2014

Library of Congress Catalog Card Number 2013952829
ISBN 978-0-7636-7306-2

14 15 16 17 18 19 TTP 10 9 8 7 6 5 4 3 2 1

Printed in Huizhou, Guangdong, China

This book was typeset in Aunt Mildred.
The illustrations were done in pencil and colored digitally.

Candlewick Press
99 Dover Street
Somerville, Massachusetts 02144

visit us at www.candlewick.com

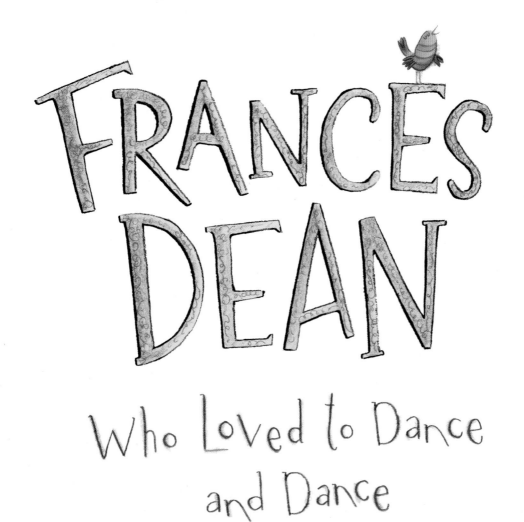

FRANCES DEAN

Who Loved to Dance and Dance

BIRGITTA SIF

CANDLEWICK PRESS

Once there was a girl
whose name was Frances Dean.
She loved to dance and dance.

At school sometimes, when no one was watching, she danced with her fingers on her desk. Or she gently tapped her toes to the beat of her teacher's voice.

But mostly she couldn't wait to go outside and dance!

When no one was around,
she would feel the wind
and dance . . .

and hear the singing of the birds
and dance and dance and dance.

But when people were around,
all she could feel were their
eyes on her ...

and she forgot how to dance.

Then one day
the birds,

who always loved
her dancing,

showed her something
unusual.

A girl, much younger than she,
was singing the most beautiful song.

Frances Dean found herself
humming along.

That night Frances Dean couldn't sleep.
She couldn't stop thinking about the
little girl and how she had shared her
beautiful song.

Frances Dean wondered if she would
ever be able to share her dance moves
like that.

The next morning when she awoke,
Frances Dean felt the wind and heard
the singing of the birds.

And she was reminded with all her heart
how much she loved to dance and dance.

So while no one was around,
she practiced her dance moves.

And when she was ready,
she let the wind move her.

And, shyly, she asked the birds,

"Can I show you my dance?"

She asked her cat, "Do you know how to dance like this?"

She even did a jig with the neighbor's dog.

And when she met the old lady in the square,
she showed her how to do the twist.

Later on, the little girl
with the beautiful song
asked Frances Dean,
"Can you show me how to
dance, too?"

And she did.

Once there was a girl
whose name was Frances Dean.
She loved to dance and dance
and dance.